Blanche McManus

The Quaker Colony

Blanche McManus

The Quaker Colony

ISBN/EAN: 9783337403546

Printed in Europe, USA, Canada, Australia, Japan

Cover: Foto ©Andreas Hilbeck / pixelio.de

More available books at **www.hansebooks.com**

The
Quaker Colony

Penned and Pictured
by
Blanche McManus

New York
E. R. Herrick & Co.
70 Fifth Avenue

COLONIAL MONOGRAPHS

THE QUAKER COLONY

INTRODUCTION

The colony of William Penn thrived and prospered solely through the efforts of the founder and the justness of the principles which he avowed.

The final outcome and growth was but to have been expected when is considered the principle involved:

As a congregation "The Society of Friends" sought a new home like unto the Pilgrims who came to Plymouth, that they might find a haven for their church.

Persecution and oppression had but spurred them on to establish their faith; it could not fail to advance and prosper, provided they were not antagonized, nor subjected to adverse circumstances or conditions, and so, they were assured by the power vested in the proprietary rights of William Penn.

That they should have secured the aid and influence of one so steadfast and honest as this brave man, was indeed fortunate; and to his earnest effort and financial aid is due the credit of that which even right and enthusiasm often availeth not.

The later attributes of the colony, and of "The City of Brotherly Love" in particular, but reaffirm the assurance that the colony was founded upon lines which bespoke from the start equality and liberality, and in which the city of Philadelphia to-day, occupies and sustains a place unique among cities throughout the world, as a city of homes and homemakers.

The distress and troublous visitations of the infant Colony were not by any means infrequent, nor did they, in any sense, lack severity, but throughout its career the perplexities were the comparatively peaceful ones of finance and territorial boundaries and rights, and warfare, riot and bloodshed were conspicuous only by their absence, which in view of the principles of justness and equality professed by the Quakers made of the Red Man a friend instead of a foe.

As prominent as was the religious feeling and motives of the " Friends," they sought not to coerce liberty and freedom of conscience in others, but rather to encourage a union wherein freedom of religion and a simple avowal of Christianity was all that was required of the community.

B. McM.

Contents

The Society of Friends

The Society of Friends, or Quakers, was founded by George Fox, a native of Drayton, in Leicestershire, England, about the middle of the seventeenth century: from the moment of the inception of the society, the members thereof were subjected to dire oppression, indignity and persecution, by fines, whipping and imprisonment.

The sect immediately grew in numbers, not in England alone, but in Ireland, Wales and Holland, to which country they had emigrated, as had the Puritans, in order to be able to freely avow their religious opinions.

They were a quiet and peaceable people, and for them to have been so unmercifully treated by all differing from their faith seems an unpardonable injustice, but at that time the Govern-

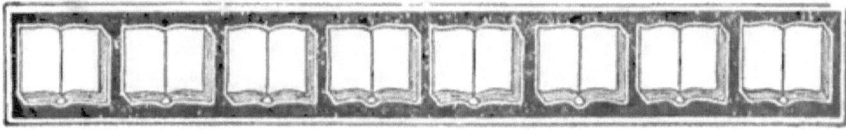

ment frowned upon any and all dissenting faiths, particularly if they sought to publicly proclaim their views.

They adopted certain strict views of equality, refused to take oath or to bow the head, to enlist as soldiers, and had no printed prayers nor hired preachers; practised simplicity in food and costume, and addressed all persons as thee and thou, and, perhaps not the least aggravation of all, to the ceremonious court itself, refused to uncover the head when in the presence of Royalty.

These omissions and lapses did much towards magnifying their unpopularity, and as they rapidly gained converts to their faith in England they were likewise vigilantly suppressed; such a democratic state of affairs was

not allowed to gain a vantage under a monarchical form of government.

The "Friends" first came to America in 1656, to the Massachusetts Bay Colony, where even among the Puritans, who had migrated and settled in the new land avowing a like principle in their demands for freedom of religious opinion, they were imprisoned, banished, and in the event of their return, as was actually the case in four instances, hanged; an uncharitableness hard to reconcile to any recognized form of the world's religion of the present day.

From this time on their numbers grew largely, and settlers of the faith were to be found scattered throughout Massachusetts, Rhode Island, Long Island, Virginia, and East and West

Jersey. These were constantly increased by the arrival of many adherents from Great Britain and the Continent.

They were generally admitted to have been thrifty and excellent citizens, full of compassion and brotherly love. They were never known to return a blow, but righteously turned the other cheek, seeming mostly to arouse the ire of their opponents from their apparent indifference to the qualities of courage and allegiance to the laws and customs of the land, attributes which were great factors in the social and moral life of the day.

It is not entirely known as to how the name Quaker originated. One authority states that it was given to them in derision of their "trembling

under the awful sense of the infinite purity of God," while Fox himself, who, as he was brought up before the magistrates to answer the charges preferred against him, told them to "quake at the name of the Lord;" either one of which explanations seems plausible and pertinent enough to be accepted.

In 1670 an order was signed by the Archbishop of Canterbury and thirteen others, directing Christopher Wrenn to pull down the Quaker meeting-houses in Ratcliffe and Horsely, which was done, the material sold and the proceeds confiscated.

Up to 1700 it is on record that individual members of the Society had been fined in the aggregate an amount equalling one million

pounds, and at one time there were over four thousand Quakers imprisoned in England and the provinces.

In numbers the sect never exceeded two hundred thousand at any time, and at the present day the orthodox Quakers probably do not exceed one hundred and twenty-five thousand, the greater part of whom are in the United States.

William Penn—Quaker

William Penn, grandson of Sir Giles Penn, an English consul in the Mediterranean, and son of Admiral Sir William Penn, the conqueror of the Island of Jamaica, was born in London, in the parish of St. Catherines, near the Tower, October 14, 1644.

As a young man, while yet a student at Oxford, he became affiliated with the Quakers, some of whom he had met and had associated with in England and Ireland; he preached in the streets of London, and was apprehended upon a warrant from the Lord Mayor, and committed to Newgate Prison; at his trial at the Old Bailey he courageously and heroically pleaded his own cause, resulting in his final acquittal.

Penn's personality was an important factor

in his success as a leader among his fellow
"Friends;" he was a cultivated and polished gentle-
man; had travelled much; was versed in law
and philosophy, and had proved himself also a
strong and forceful writer; having put forth some
valuable thoughts on his favorite subject while
in Newgate, notably: "The Great Case of Liberty
and Conscience," "An Apology for the Quakers,"
and "Truth Rescued from Imposture."

After travelling on the continent for some
months he returned to England and joined the
"Society of Friends" in 1668; almost immediately
thereafter he was incarcerated in the Tower of
London for the offence of seeking to open and
arouse heresy and treason against the edict of
the established law.

)ne of the direct causes of his imprisonment was the authorship of a work entitled "The Sandy Foundation Shaken," which embodied religious principles and criticism at direct variance with those of the land.

While in prison awaiting trial he further wrote "No Cross No Crown," and "Innocency with the Open Face," a vindication of the views and beliefs for which he had been imprisoned; his final release was brought about by royal clemency, his family always having stood high in the favor of the Royal House.

Penn inherited from his father a claim to a debt of sixteen thousand pounds against the government, which was settled by a grant of woodland in America, of forty thousand square miles,

west of the Delaware River. This circumstance
served the government a twofold purpose, that
of cancelling the debt on particularly advan-
tageous terms, and of ridding the country of a
vigorous dissenter; as Penn was desirous of
founding a colony of Quakers in the New World
where they might evolve and further develop the
ideas of religious liberty and sincerity with
which they became imbued.

Penn was chartered Lord Proprietor of the
colony in 1681, and immediately sent over his
emissary and agent, William Markham, to
acquaint the then present Swedish, Dutch and
English settlers in the locality of the anticipated
movement.

Markham, who was a cousin of Penn, was

"deputized to call a council of nine, he to preside; to read his letter and commission and the King's declaration to the inhabitants, and to take their acknowledgment of his authority and propriety; to settle boundaries between Penn and his neighbors; to survey, set out, rent, or sell lands according to the instructions given; to erect courts, appoint sheriffs, justices of the peace, etc.; to call to his aid any of the inhabitants, for the legal suppression of tumult."

After his (Markham's) arrival in the wilderness he reported in a letter sent home, thus:

". . . . it is a very fine country, if it were not so overgrown with woods, and very healthy, here people live to be a hundred years of age.

" Provisions of all sorts are indifferent plenti-

ful, venison especially, I have seen four buck bought for less than five shillings."

"The Indians kill them only for their skins, and if the Christians will not buy the flesh they let it hang and rot upon the tree. In the winter there is mighty plenty of wild fowl of all sorts. Partridges I am cloyed with, we catch them by hundreds at a time. In the fall of the leaf or after Harvest, here are abundance of wild turkeys which are mighty easy to be shot, Duck, Mallard, Geese and Swans in abundance, wild fish are in great plenty. In short, if a country life be liked by any it might be here." . . . .

Penn wished to call the colony New Wales, it being a hilly country, like that across the sea, but the King chose to name it in honor of Penn's

father, the great Admiral. Penn afterwards referred to it as Sylvania, which was promptly prefixed with P-e-n-n by the King, somewhat against the opposition of Penn, who feared it might be looked upon as a vanity in him rather than as a compliment from the King.

Having completed all his arrangements, Penn wrote an affectionate letter to his wife and children, and another "to all faithful friends in England," and immediately set sail on board the ship Welcome, accompanied by about one hundred persons, mostly "Friends" from Sussex.

After a voyage of two months they came in sight of the Delaware capes on the twenty-fourth of October; of the one hundred who took passage with Penn, thirty died of small-pox dur-

ing the voyage, another great oppression which
did not in the least, however, deter the remainder
from fulfilling their purpose.

Before embarking upon "The Holy Experi-
ment," as he was pleased to call it, Penn told the
King that he would purchase equity in the lands
of the Indians, saying that even the right of
discovery and occupation would not allow them
to usurp or take unbidden the land from its
rightful owners, the red-men.

New England had begun by trying to convert
the Indians, and had acquired a great measure of
their lands in the name of the gospel: not so with
William Penn; he avowed that the Indians were
the descendants of the ten dispersed tribes of
Israel and met them in a free and equal manner.

He argued thus: "For their original I am
ready to believe them of the Jewish race, I
mean of the stock of the ten tribes, and that
for the following reasons: First, they were to
go to a land not planted or known, hence,
across the sea.... next I find them of a like
countenance, but this is not all; they agree in
rites and reckon by moons; they have a sort of
feast of tabernacles; and are said to lay their
altar upon twelve stones, and remain in mourn-
ing a year."

As by the terms of the treaty he agreed to
occupy no lands except as might be acquired by
fair purchase, and in addition required of them
that they sell to no one except him (Penn) or his
agents. This proposition, in view, perhaps, of

the way in which the matter was led up to, was readily assented to on their part.

Upon Penn's arrival at Newcastle on the Delaware, where the settlement had been planted by his Secretary, Markham, who had preceded him, he was received with due honor and ceremony as befitted his position as Lord Proprietor of the colony.

The original charter vested William Penn with a perpetual proprietorship of a vast region which included what was afterward set apart as Delaware, in consideration of Penn's having given a receipt in full to the King for the amount of his claim on the Government, and an honorarium of two beaver skins per annum.

Penn sought to found the colony on the basis

of religious freedom and declared that every
Christian without distinction of sect should be
eligible to public employment and recognition,
and that it was to afford an asylum to the good
and oppressed of all nations, with a frame of government which would be an example, showing all
men as free and happy as they could be.

After certain minor details had been adjusted
Penn immediately sought to consummate the
treaty with the Indians which he had so earnestly
wished for and avowed.

The Charter comprehended a much more
extensive tract than they were prepared to barter
for at once but agreed then and there that all of
the land ultimately to be occupied should only be
taken up and acquired by direct purchase.

As in all things he counselled that justice and moderation, so consistent with his own peaceful views and acts.

The great treaty was made at the Indian village of Shackamaxon, on the Delaware, in November of the same year as Penn's advent in the colony, and was set forth in terms which meant something more than the mere price of lands: "The recognition of equal rights of humanity."

Plans were immediately begun for the laying out of the city of Philadelphia, which Penn, true to his principles of brotherly love, so named after the ancient Greek city of Asia Minor.

The land was surveyed and the plans drawn by Thomas Holme, the Surveyor-General, the

streets being named after the different varieties
of trees to be found in the vicinity, and crossing
each other at regular intervals, dividing the city
into broad squares.

Such of the land as was early occupied, was
built up with frame houses, each in the centre of
its own plot of ground, which soon afterward
gave way to the more substantial brick and stone,
so familiar in the older buildings of the city yet
to be seen; the city thus earning and meriting
early in its career a reputation for fitness and
conformity, the fame of which has since been so
well sustained.

After certain intermediate changes, over
which Penn himself presided, and ably dealt
with, the question of an extension of Crown

Privileges and the settlement of the boundary
line between Maryland and Pennsylvania came
up, and necessitated his return to England in
order to the better deal with the subject. He
sailed therefor in 1684, leaving behind a prosperous and flourishing colony of seven thousand
souls.

While in England he met with sundry diffi-
culties, and still further annoyance and indifference on the part of the authorities, although
finally through the intercession of his friend, the
King, his claims were recognized and adjusted
and he further secured the release of some twelve
hundred of his fellow Quakers who were at the
time imprisoned in England; an action which was
the forerunner of a proclamation by the King

himself, which resulted in the granting of the liberty of conscience and freedom of religion to all.

Penn was readily able to bring about a settlement of the dispute in reference to the Maryland boundary line, which resulted in Lord Baltimore accepting a tract which was about one-half the extent of the original claim.

In 1692, and while Penn was still in England, the authorities accused him of disloyalty, and sought to abrogate his powers by taking away his proprietorship rights in the colony, and by a Royal Commission the governing power was transferred and vested in the English Governor of New York; these suspicions were soon after dissipated, and the proprietorship restored to Penn, which was held by his direct descendants

until the breaking out of the Revolution.

During Penn's absence in England the government was in the control of Thomas Lloyd, who was not a Quaker, but who was esteemed and trusted highly by Penn and his associates. Penn did not return again to America until 1699, during which time the local government changed from hand to hand in the person of the Governor many times, but always in support of the original ideas of the founder to the fullest possible extent.

After his return to this country Penn occupied the slate-roofed house which remained standing on the original site on Second Street, between Chestnut and Walnut, well within the memory of many now living.

He remained in this country but for the brief period of two years, and in 1701 again returned to England; he had hardly arrived in London when false charges of a claim were preferred against him which he refused to pay; accordingly he was cast into the Fleet, where he contracted an acute disease. His position was finally vindicated and he was released, but his health grew rapidly worse, and paralysis deprived him of his memory and of the power of locomotion.

After his release from prison he lived for six years, afflicted with much personal suffering, during which time his business affairs were ably managed and conducted by his wife. He died at Ruscombe, in Berkshire, July 30, 1718.

Here had been a nature of strong contrasting

emotions, a shepherd of a flock, a courtier, a religious enthusiast, and an able man of business, beginning life as the son and heir of one who was high in the favor of the court, and finally becoming the leader of a despised, persecuted, and humble sect, still retaining the favor and intimacy of the court itself, although avowing at the time doctrines which other of the authorities would not willingly have overlooked.

He had given his all, representing his fortune, enthusiasm, the best years of his life, and his most earnest effort, for the good of the colony, with the result that the settlement proved to be, in his own words, " . . . the greatest colony that ever man established in America on a private credit, and the most prosperous beginnings that

are to be found therein . . ."

Relief as to the serenity of the affairs of the province came too late to ease the condition of the honest and generous founder's mind or purse; but his former interests, after a protracted law-suit, finally passed to the children of his second wife, who with their immediate descendants remained in close proprietorship until the War of the Revolution.

The Quaker Colony

The founding of Pennsylvania emanated solely from the wish of William Penn to establish "a free colony for all mankind."

His inheritance of a claim upon the then ruling house of Great Britain was but the means to an end.

The charter which conveyed to William Penn this tract of wilderness was not enough in his honest eyes to establish a permanent claim and title to the land which descended unto him. He sought by terms of purchase and the famous treaty to build a firm foundation for the fame and faith of his religion.

Previous to the second English occupation of New York the Dutch territory in America extended from the Connecticut River on the east to

the Delaware River on the west, all of which was then peopled largely by the Dutch themselves.

After the Dutch possessions fell into English hands in 1664, the Duke of York gave to Lord John Berkley and Sir George Carteret the tract lying between the Hudson and Delaware Rivers.

Carteret had been Governor of the Island of Jersey in the English Channel, and named the new proprietory province New Jersey, which was further subdivided into East and West Jersey and governed by Carteret and Berkley respectively.

Berkley disposed of West Jersey to the Quakers, and after the death of Carteret, Penn purchased from his heirs the eastern division.

The province of Delaware, named for De la Warre, the Governor of Virginia, belonged prop-

44

erly to the Duke of York as proprietor, but Penn's rule governed there, he being the Duke's tenant.

The Dutch claimed jurisdiction over the waters of Delaware Bay and River, which claim was assailed by the Swedes who had migrated there and settled at Wiaco under the leadership of New Amsterdam's disgruntled former Governor, Peter Minuit, in 1638.

The redoubtable Stuyvesant set out against them in 1655 with a formidable force by sea and land; subdued them and was able to substantiate his claim until the fall of Dutch rule in America in 1674.

In 1681 William Penn's charter secured him the proprietorship of forty thousand square miles of territory, a portion of which was afterwards

made over to Maryland as a compromise of the claims of Charles Calvert, the third Lord Baltimore, that Penn's grant encroached upon his own territory.

Fifty years later this was further compromised, and led up to the running of a new and permanent boundary line by Mason and Dixon in 1767, the boundary posts having on one side the arms of William Penn, and on the other those of Lord Baltimore.

This was the famous Mason and Dixon line which so strongly marked the limits of the North and South in the late Civil War, which speaks much for its strategic value and importance.

Previous to Penn's arrival in the colony, only the seat of government, as represented by the

courts and offices, was at Newcastle on the Delaware, and here Penn was first introduced to his new possessions.

The settlement at that time was principally occupied by the Dutch, by whom it was founded, with a sprinkling of Swedes, Germans, Welsh and English.

Later Penn moved up the river in his ship to the Swedish settlement of Uplands, which he promptly renamed Chester, in honor of a number of persons from that locality at home who had joined the expedition.

.As soon thereafter as practicable, was consummated the Treaty with the Indians, so famously pictured by Benjamin West, and a Frame of Government for the colony was adopted.

At this time was also enacted a code called the Great Law, defining minutely the rights of citizens, and which only required of them that they should put all faith in Jesus Christ, in consideration of which all further toleration was granted.

It was, of course, implied that all were to hold themselves peaceably and justly in civil society. The only offences which were especially to be discouraged were: "drinking healths, prizes, stage plays, and cards and dice;" but the criminal code was mild in the extreme, only murder being punishable by death.

The year following Penn's arrival over fifteen hundred settlers arrived from England, mostly Quakers, and still others yet from Germany who

had also embraced the religion of the Friends, and who ultimately settled at Germantown, now a part of the present city of Philadelphia.

Penn wished to establish a Christian state, founded on Christian principles, and directed by Christian love, principles and aims, which was quite the opposite of the blue-laws of Plymouth Colony and the regime of warfare and conquest in Virginia, the scenes of England's other activities in the new world.

In spite of the process of warfare and bloodshed, through which the Virginia Colony had gone, it had in a way been more favored than the other English settlements in America, and was more than usually productive and resourceful, the climate was equable, and woods

and waters abounded with fish and fowl. With direct deep-water communication with England the export trade was in flourishing condition; this was the state of affairs which the Quakers looked forward to in being able to locate their colony in a contiguous and adjacent spot. To some extent this proved ultimately to be, particularly in reference to the desirability of the location, though the settlers were more taken up with the founding of their colony than they were with the immediate establishment of commercial relations, the project being endowed with sufficient means to launch itself on a prosperous wave at the start.

The success of the Quaker colony was a victory of peace and a triumph of the noble virtues

of innocency and truth as against selfishness, warfare and mercenary motives, which have so often overruled these finer instincts.

For nearly one hundred years the colony was under the direct control of the Friends, and during that time no war-cry was to be heard within its confines—"Quaker garb had proven as invulnerable as a coat of mail."

The colony was early and ever noted for its high moral character, good order, peace, and an intense love of faith; and fitting it was that the Declaration of Independence should have reached perfection on the same spot where was so earnestly avowed and practised the principles of freedom and equality.

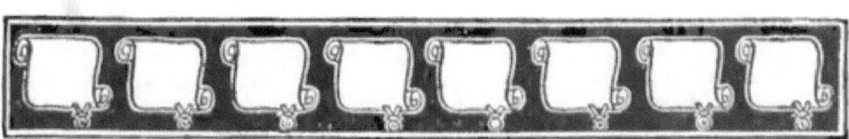

The Great Treaty

Any account of Penn's Treaty with the Indians must depend very greatly upon traditional reports of the circumstance, little having been written in reference thereto and no records are available which recount the actual happenings of the occasion, beyond such as are to be found in documents relating to contemporary events, and of the conditions which made the treaty desirable.

In spite of the absence of documentary evidence of the details of the conference, we are in possession of a sufficient amount of verified fact to assure us of the probability of the generally accepted version being correct.

The Treaty was made late in November, 1682, at Shackamaxon, some miles above the set-

tlement, on the Delaware River, but now included within the limits of the present city of Philadelphia.

Penn, accompanied by his council, interpreters, and a delegation of the curious Dutch, Swedish and English settlers, came up the river to the appointed meeting place, and the Governor's barge moored to the bank opposite the great elm, beneath which burned the council fires of the red men.

A peaceful and romantic scene, which was further heightened by the picturesque surroundings, and the wealth of color and splendor with which Nature herself endowed the occasion.

The Indians were represented at the treaty by delegates from three nations, the Delawares,

Iroquois, and Shawnese, with probably a scattering from the other neighborhood tribes.

They were drawn up in a great circle beneath the shadow of the elm, a representative horde of noble red men, the Chiefs in the centre, surrounded by their councillors and braves, with the squaws and their papooses in the background.

In their midst sat Chief Tamanen, the great Sachem of the Delawares, gorgeous with dye and feathers. He was their great prophet and adviser, and was supposed to be in close alliance with the Great and Good Spirit and highly endowed with wisdom, virtue, and prudence.

As the Quakers appeared upon the scene, the contrast between the two races was made the

more apparent.

The Founders were attired in their quaint gray costumes, with coats extending to the knees, and well becovered with buttons, ample waistcoats, knee breeches, buckled shoes, and ruffles at the neck and sleeves. Penn's dress was distinguishable from the others only by a sash of blue silk which he wore around the body, while his secretary, Markham, wore the prescribed dress of the English service.

On the head of the great Sachem was a chaplet, a decorative headpiece which held up a small deer-horn, the emblem of kingly dignity and power, and which, when worn, was understood to sanctify the locality and the persons of all present inviolable. He smoked the Calumet, or Pipe

of Peace, a long pipe of hard black wood and
wound with ribbon and coral interspersed with
feathers of various hues.

The treaty was to be an everlasting covenant
of peace and friendship between the two races;
in strong contrast with the agreements that had
been made in other parts of the country, notably
that of Carver, of the Plymouth colony, whose
treaty with Massasoit comprehended nothing
more than a defensive war alliance.

The treaty of William Penn was never broken
or overreached by either party thereto, so far as
the respective organizations were concerned.

Through the interpreters Penn addressed
them thus:

"We meet on the broad pathway of good

faith and good will; no advantage shall be taken by either side, and all shall be openness and love.

"I will not call you children, for parents sometimes chide their children; nor brother, for brothers differ. The friendship between you and me I will not compare to a chain, for that the rains might rust, or a falling tree might break.

"We are all the same as if one man's body was to be divided into two parts; we are all one flesh and blood."

After these, and probably still other expressions of friendliness, Penn unrolled the parchment on which were written the details of the plans set forth in the preliminary address, presented it to the Sachems, and desired of them to preserve it carefully for three generations, that

their children might know what had passed between them.

Little more is recorded or known, except
that presents and peace offerings passed between
them, and the Indians, who had previously laid
down their arms, presented to the Quakers a belt
of wampum, the official pledge of fidelity, and in
reply said :

"We will live in love and concord with William Penn and his children as long as the sun
and moon shall endure."

This was ever afterward lived up to, and no
Indian ever knowingly or wilfully shed Quaker
blood.

There, facing the golden autumn sunset, was
concluded the most momentous deed which had

yet taken place between the invaders of the red man's domain and its natural and rightful owners, and of which more has been said in praise than of any other like incident transmitted to posterity.

This, says Voltaire, was the only agreement between those people and the Christians which was not ratified by an oath, or never broken, which led him to further express himself to the effect that the religion of William Penn was the nearest approach to accepted Christianity.

It is greatly to the honor and glory of all concerned that the manifest expressions of peace and good will so overshadowed those of mercenary trade and barter.

Romance and tradition also surrounded the famous Treaty Elm for many years. It became

famous again during the Revolution; the English General Simcoe so respecting it that when his soldiers were about to fell it for firewood, he placed a sentinel beneath with instructions to allow not a branch of it to be touched.

Certain other conditions and agreements were entered into from time to time, all bearing more or less directly upon the promises that had been exchanged at the time of the Treaty; one of importance in reference to trial by jury, wherein it was agreed that whenever an Indian was to be tried for any offence within the jurisdiction of the Quakers the panel was to be composed of six Indians and six white men.

On a certain occasion when a purchase of land was being arranged for, it was stipulated that for

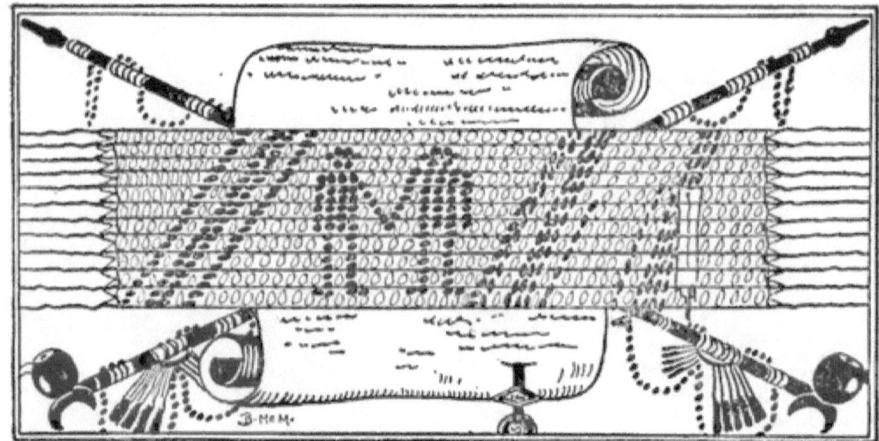

the price to be paid the Indians were to give in exchange as large a tract as could be traversed in a three days' walk on either side of a square. After a rather deliberate stroll of only a day and a half's duration, including stops, the Quakers concluded that they had covered enough ground for their needs, and left the remainder of their due in the hands of the Indians, bespeaking great confidence in the business integrity on the part of all concerned.

The City of Brotherly Love

Before setting out from England Penn published an account of his province, with the intention of attracting settlers thereto. He promised to sell five thousand acres of ground, free from incumbrance, for One Hundred Pounds, with a quit-rent of a shilling yearly for one hundred acres. He offered to rent lands, not exceeding two hundred acres in each tract, at one penny yearly per acre, and to make an allowance for servants carried over to the amount of fifty acres per head.

Further conditions were set forth and agreed, viz.: "that so soon as it pleaseth the persons who arrive there, a certain quantity of land or ground plat shall be laid out for a large Town or City, in the most convenient place upon the river

for health and navigation; and every purchaser and adventurer shall by lot have so much land therein as shall answer to the proportion which he hath bought or taken up on rent."

As early as May, 1682, before Penn's arrival upon the scene, Thomas Holme, with others, began the laying out of the great town. Penn's instructions were "to settle the figure of the town so that the streets may hereafter be uniform down to the water, and let every house be placed, if the person pleases, in the middle of its plat, so that there may be ground on each side for gardens or orchards."

According to the original plan, there was a street leading from the Delaware to the Schuylkill River, and a boundary street lying along each

river. Originally these streets bore different
names from those which they do at present, but
the nomenclature was early changed in favor of
the present form, that of naming them after the
local varieties of trees.

The name Philadelphia was chosen by the proprietor himself, and was probably adopted from
that of the ancient city of the Old World, the seat
of one of the early Christian churches, signifying
brotherly love, which naturally commended itself
to the taste and judgment of the founder, who
fondly spoke of it thus:

"And thou, Philadelphia, the virgin settlement of this province, named before thou wert
born, what love, what care, what service, what
travail, has there been to bring thee forth and

preserve thee from such as would defile thee."

The city increased greatly within the next few months, within a year it being estimated that there were eighty dwellings and over five hundred inhabitants, and in 1700, twenty years after, there were over seven hundred houses and forty-five hundred inhabitants.

In the slate-roofed house before mentioned was born John Penn, the only child of the family who was born in America. William Penn, Jr., came to the country in 1704, and was said to be no credit to his illustrious father in taste or habits.

Germantown, now incorporated in the city of Philadelphia, was settled by the German Quakers who came over early in the beginnings of the

colony. The location was first called to the attention of Francis Daniel Pastorius, a personal friend of William Penn (Whittier's "Pennsylvania Pilgrim").

The tract comprised nearly six thousand acres, and was peopled mostly by fellow-countrymen of Pastorius, although not all of them were of the Quaker persuasion. Here was established the first type foundry in America, by Christopher Sower, in 1735, who also published the first quarto German Bible.

The facts recounted herein follow closely the actual occurrences and events which led up to the founding and the successful conduct of the "Quaker Colony"; and to the individual whose sterling qualities and admirable foresight which made

this possible, all honor and respect is due.

The trials and vicissitudes which befel the colony were purely akin to the principles which founded it, and were not the usual causes of bloodshed, riot, and warfare with which other of the colonies were afflicted, and, above all, a fact which added not a little to their serenity, was the complete pacification of the Indian, who became a friend instead of a foe.

Here also is the complete ascendency of the home-making, fellow-loving qualities so often lacking in colony-building; not but that their troubles were at times grave and difficult to deal with. But, to reiterate, it pleased these generous people to deal kindly, rather than to attempt the persuasion of anger, or warring words and acts.